BENJI FRANKLIN

KID ZILLIONAIRE

Money Troubles

Stone Arch Books
a Capstone Imprint

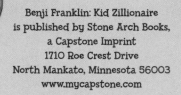

Benji Franklin: Kid Zillionaire
is published by Stone Arch Books,
a Capstone Imprint
1710 Roe Crest Drive
North Mankato, Minnesota 56003
www.mycapstone.com

Cataloging-in-Publication Data is available on
the Library of Congress website.
ISBN: 978-1-4965-0369-5 (paper over board)
ISBN: 978-1-4965-2309-9 (eBook)
ISBN: 978-1-4965-4137-6 (paperback)

Summary: Benji Franklin is the world's go-to genius. He's
already saved the planet twice before, and now he's at it
again. With the help of his extraordinary problem-solving
skills (and a solid gold submarine), he'll be busy stopping
dangerous underwater earthquakes and catching
outer-space cyber criminals! But with balancing saving
the world and doing his homework, are there some
problems too challenging for even the Kid Zillionaire?

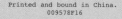

Printed and bound in China.
009578F16

BENJI FRANKLIN

KID ZILLIONAIRE

FRANKLIN

written by
Raymond Bean

illustrated by
Matthew Vimislik

CHAPTER 1
I'd Love to Chat, But . . .

When I invented the world-famous Excuse Yourself app, I made it for kids. I didn't expect so many adults to want to use it too. But my data shows that more adults use Excuse Yourself than kids! It's not very helpful to them, of course, because it's designed to solve everyday kids' problems, like forgetting homework or "accidentally" feeding the dog your lunch. Stuff like that.

I thought about creating an adult version of Excuse Yourself but figured it would probably be totally boring creating an app that helps adults get out of work, paying bills, and whatever else adults do. Also, I don't have the time. Since creating Excuse Yourself, I've been super busy. It seems like every time there's a catastrophe about to happen that adults can't figure out, they want my help.

But I'm not complaining. I've built a business helping the world's most successful people get out of some of the world's most dangerous situations.

I don't mean to brag, but I'm what you might call superhero-ish. I don't have a cape or a costume or anything like that, but I know how to save the day.

When I got the call for my latest mission, I was at lunch. It was pretty bad timing because Cindy Meyers—the biggest pain in the rump at my school—was sitting directly across from me. We're allowed to have phones at school, but we're not supposed to take calls, so I put in my earbuds to make it look like I was only listening to music.

It was a video call, and I recognized the number. I clicked the answer icon, and Sir Robert appeared on my screen.

"Good afternoon, Master Franklin!"

I nodded without saying anything.

"You seem a bit stiff, lad. Are you all right?" asked Sir Robert.

I nodded again. Cindy was staring right at me, arms crossed.

"I see you talking on your phone, Benji Franklin," she said, taking out her own phone. "I'm emailing this to the principal. So I suggest you hang up." Cindy is in charge of the school Decency Committee. She's always on the lookout for kids breaking the rules. For some reason, she seems to be everywhere I go.

"I can't talk right now," I whispered to Sir Robert. "I'm going to get in trouble."

"Nonsense!" he insisted. "Something's come up that requires your immediate attention."

"I'm at lunch right now," I told him, "and I'm really going to get into trouble if I keep talking."

"Don't be absurd. I'll contact your principal and let her know you're needed straight away."

I smiled, clicked speaker, removed the earbuds, and glancing at Cindy, said, "Can you repeat that last part, Sir Robert? I didn't hear you clearly."

"I said, you're not going to get in any trouble. I'll contact your principal and let her know you're needed urgently," repeated Sir Robert.

Cindy stuck out her tongue.

"Now kindly stop showing off and take me off speaker," he said. I did and he went on. "I received a call from an associate of mine who finds himself in an explosive situation. I suggested he contact you."

"What's the problem?" I asked.

"I wish it were that simple, Benji," Sir Robert explained. "It's more like PROBLEMS. He'll give you a call and provide the location. You'll need to get there as soon as possible. Use your spaceship, and don't forget to bring that new submarine of yours."

I'd purchased my new submarine a few weeks earlier. I had it painted solid gold with tangerine orange lightning bolts on the sides. It's designed to go to the deepest parts of the ocean, and it's stuffed with the best technology available.

"It sounds like fun," I said, "but you'd better call my mom and dad and make sure it's okay that I go."

"Already done. Your bags are being packed as we speak. Have a safe journey. Over and out."

"You think you're such a big shot!" Cindy shouted as I hung up.

"People get in trouble, and they call on me to save the day. I'm like Batman," I growled.

My phone rang. "Excuse me, as much as I'd love to stay and chat," I told Cindy, "I have to take this."

I walked out of the cafeteria, into the hall, and stopped at a door that read "storage." I glanced over my shoulder to make sure no one was watching. The closet was locked, but when I held my hand over the word *storage*, a scanner recognized my fingerprints and unlocked it. I closed the door behind me and answered the call.

"Benji Franklin here. How can I help?" I whispered. I'd converted the storage closet into my private office a few weeks earlier. Every superhero needs a hideout or secret place to escape for a while.

A nervous voice on the other end of the phone said, "Sir Robert told me to call. I need your help."

I walked farther into my nest, sat at my desk, and turned on the computer. Several screens blinked to life. "What's the problem?" I asked.

"I can't explain now. I'll email you my location. Please, get here as fast as possible," said the man.

"Who is this?" I asked.

The call started breaking up, and I heard a loud rumbling in the background. "It's happening again! Please get here as soon as you can, before this place blows up and —"

The call dropped, and he was gone. I tried to call him back a few times, but I couldn't get through.

I leaned back in my chair thinking about what the man had said. I wondered what the rumbling noise was in the background and what he meant when he said the place might blow up. It sounded pretty dangerous and intense. I couldn't wait to get to work.

The only person who knew about my secret hideaway was Mrs. Petty, the school principal. She agreed to let me use it as long as I didn't tell the other kids. Mrs. Petty has been really cool about letting me miss school when I have a mission. I just have to make sure to get my class work done too, which has been a bit of a challenge.

Sir Robert doesn't think I should even go to school anymore. He thinks I should focus on my business, but my mom and dad want me to be like other kids my age and go to school.

"Location received," the computer said.

"Thanks, Saunders. Where are we headed?" I asked excitedly.

Saunders is my digital assistant. He's a super-intelligent computer program loaded into all my electronics. He's always there when I need him.

A map of the world appeared on the screen. A location blinked in the middle of the Atlantic Ocean.

"I'll send for the car," Saunders said. "Don't forget to check in with Mrs. Petty before leaving early."

CHAPTER 2
Saddle Up

About ten minutes later, Mrs. Petty and I stood at the back of the school waiting for my car to pick me up early. It's one of the perks of being a zillionaire. I don't have to wait for my parents to drive me from place to place. I have a chauffeur.

"I'll have someone contact you with the assignments you'll need to make up while you're away," Mrs. Petty said. "How long will you be gone?"

"I don't know," I said.

"Have your parents give me a call once you know the details," she requested.

"Will do," I said as the limo pulled up.

"You'd think you were a secret agent or the president the way you're whisked around the world," Mrs. Petty said.

"I like to think of myself as more of a superhero type," I reminded her.

"Just make sure you get your work done, Mr. Superhero." She smiled.

My driver, Mr. Kensington, opened the limo's door. Kensington used to work for Sir Robert, but he was the driver on my first mission and has been with me ever since.

As we headed to our first destination, I tried calling Sir Robert again, but he still didn't answer.

"Do you know where Sir Robert is?" I asked Kensington.

"He's on vacation, Mr. Franklin," he said.

"Yes, that's what his voicemail says, but I need to get in touch with him," I insisted.

"I'll let him know that if I hear from him, sir," said Kensington.

A few moments later, Kensington dropped me off at Mom's farm. She runs a bunch of food pantries, and all the vegetables, milk, and meat for the pantries comes from her farm. She used to struggle to have enough food to donate to people, so I bought the farm for her. She says I'm the most thoughtful son in the world. Who am I to argue?

The farm used to be a small airport. It's not only the perfect place to raise animals and grow crops, but it's also the perfect place to keep my spaceship. As far as I know, I'm the only kid in the world who owns one. Sir Robert gave it to me after I helped him out of a sticky situation. I keep it in a hangar toward the back of the farm. Mom was outside waiting for us when we pulled up.

"Your father is already down at the dock getting the submarine ready," Mom said when I got out of the limo. "I spoke with the principal, and she said it's okay if you miss a few days, but she sounded concerned about how much you've missed lately."

"I'm not worried about it," I said.

"That makes one of us," Mom replied.

"Happy travels, sir. I'll be here when you get back," Kensington said.

I slapped his hand. "Thanks for the ride. I'll see you in a few days."

"I'll look forward to it, sir," he said. "Have a wonderful adventure." His window hummed closed, and he drove off.

"Don't worry, Mom. I've got it covered. Did Dad hear anything more from Sir Robert?" I asked.

"I don't know, but it seems like you boys will be gone for a while. After this mission, I want you to take a break from all the traveling. The world will just have to learn to get on without you."

"I don't think that's possible," I said, winking.

"I have a feeling you might be right," she said.

Once in the hangar, I held my hand up to the gold BF initials on the side of the spaceship.

The hand recognition device identified me, and the glass top lifted open. Steps unfolded out of the ship. I felt like a secret agent every time I climbed in.

As I sat in the pilot's seat, the dashboard computer said, "Hello, Benji."

"Hello, Saunders," I said.

Mom climbed in too and sat in the copilot's seat. There were empty snack wrappers all over the place and a few misplaced sweatshirts lying around. "You're not going anywhere until this ship is cleaned up," she said. "How many times have I told you that you have to take good care of this spaceship?"

"Eighty times, Mrs. Franklin," Saunders said.

"Please let me handle this, Saunders," I said.

"Sorry, Mom." I pouted. "I was in here a few days ago and meant to clean up, but I forgot."

"Nice try," Saunders said.

"Thank you, Saunders, but please mind your own business," I repeated.

After a quick lecture, Mom gave me a kiss, climbed out, and I fired up the engine.

"Opening roof," Saunders said. "Prepare for takeoff."

The roof on the hangar slowly opened up. There wasn't a cloud in the sky. "Next stop, the docks," Saunders said.

The ship launched perfectly, lifting off the ground like a super-charged helicopter. It rose up out of the hangar and then blasted forward.

In minutes, we were hovering above the sub at the docks. Dad's face popped up on the dashboard screen. "Hi, son! Go ahead and attach the sub."

"Activating magnets to attach the submarine," Saunders confirmed.

I felt the magnetic field on the bottom of the ship activate. The sub started to rise from the water. It floated up slowly and in no time was firmly attached to the bottom of the ship.

"The sub is safely secured," Saunders said.

A hatch in the ship's floor lifted up, and Dad's head appeared. "Well done!" he said. "The magnets worked perfectly."

Dad had lined the bottom of the spaceship and the top of the submarine with superstrong magnets. By attaching the sub to the bottom of the ship, we could take it anywhere in the world.

Dad climbed the rest of the way up, and the hatch closed behind him. He plopped into the seat next to me and gave me a high-five.

A bunch of people stood on the other side of the docks looking like they'd just seen an alien. I gave a thumbs-up and threw the thrusters forward. We soared high above the water. Flying Saunders was pretty easy. I was in control, but he monitored everything I did. If I lost control, Saunders took over. I could also put him on autopilot, and he would take over completely.

"Where are we headed?" I asked.

"A string of islands in the middle of the Atlantic Ocean," Saunders answered. "I have the location programmed." A GPS map appeared on the screen in front of me.

"Thank you, Saunders," I said.

It would have taken a really long time to fly all the way to the Atlantic Islands in a plane. In my spaceship, we can get there tons faster, because we can fly out of Earth's atmosphere. Once out of the atmosphere, we aren't so much flying as we were orbiting. I hit the boosters, and the speed was outrageous.

Below, the Earth looked like a giant blue marble. We raced toward the line where day met night. In no time at all, we had traveled across the United States and soared high over the Atlantic Ocean.

I was having so much fun Earth-gazing that I lost track of time. Before I knew it, we were starting our descent. We were in a totally different time zone when we reentered the atmosphere. I thought about how the kids at school were probably at lunch, and I was on the other side of the planet.

"Did Sir Robert tell you anything about what we're doing here?" I asked Dad.

"He only said that it was complicated," Dad said.

We followed the GPS to what looked like a large oil platform floating several miles off the shore of a small island. We hovered above it. I could make out several smaller ships docked to the larger platform. All kinds of machinery dotted the deck, but it was hard to make out through the darkness.

"Looks like they're drilling for oil," Dad said.

"Yeah, I don't see any signs of trouble."

I called the number that had sent us the coordinates.

"Hi, it's Benji Franklin," I said to the man who answered. "We've arrived, but I need a place to land my ship."

"Are you in some kind of UFO or something?" asked the man.

"You could say that," I replied. "I also need a place to drop my sub."

"There's a small airport on the island where you can land," the man explained. "I've already notified

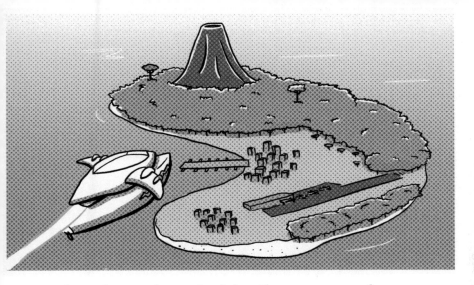

them that you've arrived, but I'm pretty sure they weren't expecting you so fast, and I know they weren't expecting a flying saucer. You can drop your sub in the small harbor near the airport."

He was still talking when the dashboard blinked. Saunders informed me that he had located the harbor and the airport.

"I've got the locations," I said. "We'll land my ship and then head out to meet you in the sub."

"Please hurry," the man said.

The island was very small and one of about a hundred that dotted the area. I could make out the lights of the small runway not far from the harbor. We lowered the ship, deactivated the magnets, and dropped the submarine into the harbor. I turned the ship and headed in the direction of the airport.

"You're looking good," Dad said. "I'd take her in slow. The runway is pretty small, and you don't want to overshoot it."

I slowed down the ship, which was a good thing because suddenly the lights of the runway vanished. And not just the runway lights, but the lights of the entire island! One minute the island was sparkling with streetlights and lights from houses, and the next it had vanished into the darkness of night as if someone had thrown a switch.

"Where'd it go?" I asked.

Dad turned on the emergency lights and flooded the ground below us with bright, white light.

"Looks like they lost power," Dad said.

Saunders switched into autopilot mode.

Thankfully we made contact with the runway and landed safely. The runway was extremely small. I saw only two other planes. Both were rusted out and looked like they hadn't been used in years.

A man waved two orange light sticks at the far end of the runway, and we drove over and parked the ship.

I opened the hatch. "What happened?" I asked. "The whole place went dark right as we were about to land."

"My apologies," he said. "We lost power again." He was a small man with a long white beard and dark eyes. He wore flip-flops, a T-shirt, and a bathing suit covered in brightly colored flowers.

"How did you lose power to the runway?" Dad asked. "Isn't there a backup?"

"We were on backup power already. We lost the backup when the earthquake hit," replied the man.

"When did you have an earthquake?" I asked.

"As you were approaching. It stopped right before you touched down," he explained.

I suddenly felt really lucky. If I had been landing as the earth was shaking that would have been really dangerous.

"I'm thankful you landed safely. Please, let me be the first to welcome to our island, Mr. Franklin."

"Thanks," Dad and I said at the same time. We did that a lot lately, now that people had started calling me Mr. Franklin too.

"I've never seen a machine like yours before. What is it?" the man asked.

"It's actually a spaceship," I said. "It's the reason we were able to get here so fast."

"You'll have to give me a tour of it sometime. Right now, we should get off this runway before another earthquake hits. I can drop you off at the docks and meet up with you later. In the meantime, I need to try to get the electricity back on."

We walked over to him and shook hands.

"Are you an electrician too?" I asked.

"No, I'm the prime minister," he said.

"If you're the prime minister, why are you landing planes?" Dad asked.

"The airport was closed for the night, and it's not every day that we have Benji Franklin visit our island. I'm honored to have you here. Sir Robert told me all about you. I've arranged for a boat to take you out to the sub you dropped in the harbor. Is there anything else you'll need from me?"

"A place to stay, and I'd appreciate it if you'd tell me a little bit about what's going on here," I said.

"It's the earthquakes. I've lived on this island my whole life and never experienced one. Now, we've had about a dozen in the last few days," he said.

"That's strange," Dad said.

"Extremely," said the prime minister. "And as much as the earthquakes have me worried, the big concern is the volcano. It's been dormant for as long as anyone can remember, but the other day, we noticed smoke billowing from the top."

"Do you know who called me for help?" I asked.

"Of course, the captain of the scientific vessel offshore. I gave them permission to map the seafloor a few months ago. As soon as the earthquakes and volcanic activity started up, I asked for their help."

"Why are they mapping the seafloor?" Dad asked.

"They're working on a study that will help preserve our beautiful underwater habitat."

"We'd better get going," I said.

The prime minister ferried us out to the sub. I'd only used the sub a few times, and I couldn't wait see what it could do. We fired up the engines and cruised out to the massive cargo ship.

CHAPTER 3
Captain?

The cargo ship was gigantic. I tied my sub up next to it, and Dad and I climbed aboard.

A man stood on the deck. He paced back and forth, chewing on his fingernails. He wore a captain's hat that looked like one you'd buy in a souvenir shop. His eyes were wide and wild.

"You must be Benji Franklin," he said. "I'm the captain." The way his eyes darted from side to side made me feel a little suspicious of him.

"Captain what?" Dad asked, shaking his hand.

"Captain is fine." He talked in a low voice, almost like a whisper.

"I appreciate you guys coming out here on such short notice," he said, looking at the ground. "I called my friend, Sir Robert, for help. And I'll be honest, I was kind of surprised when they told me he was sending a kid."

"I understand," I said. "I'm used to it."

"I thought they'd send a team of engineers or something," he added.

"Benji has a supernatural ability to solve complicated problems. You wouldn't believe some of the things he's accomplished. I'm sure if you explain what's happening, he'll be able to help," Dad said.

"You can't tell anyone what's happening here. If word got out, it would be very bad for my reputation," explained the captain.

"Helping people out of bad situations is kind of my specialty," I said. "Have you ever heard of my app, Excuse Yourself?"

He shook his head that he hadn't.

"The sooner I know what's going on, the sooner I can help you," I assured him.

"We'll have to go down for me to show you. Is

your sub designed to go to three thousand meters?"

"It can go to any depth. I've never been down as deep as three thousand meters, though. Let's do it."

We climbed back in my sub. I steered us away from the dock, and we slipped under water.

"The prime minister mentioned that you're mapping the seafloor. How many scientists are in your crew?" Dad asked.

"It's not really important," he said.

Dad and I gave each other a look. The captain's behavior seemed strange, but I couldn't figure out why. I felt more like a detective than a superhero.

"He said you and the other scientists were helping discover why they're having earthquakes and the volcano has become active," I said.

"Yeah, something like that," he said, not looking at either one of us.

I was so focused on the captain that I stopped paying attention to what I was doing. The sub was so easy to use that I had already descended almost two thousand meters below the surface. Outside, everything had gone completely black.

We descended to twenty-five hundred meters, and I noticed lights flickering in the distance. At first I thought it might be another sub, but then I realized what it was. "Bioluminescence?" I asked.

"Smart kid," the captain replied. "Yes, that light is bioluminescence. It's so dark down here that many of the creatures generate their own light."

"Now turn on your lights," the captain said.

Dad turned on the lights to reveal an underwater alien world. Massive columns rose up, chugging out black-ish water like chimneys. Crabs and other wriggling creatures covered the columns.

"Unbelievable!" Dad and I said in unison.

I cruised past a towering column. "It's a hydrothermal tube," the captain said. "There are thousands of them down here around these islands."

We cruised by a few more, each one more amazing than the next. There were sea creatures I had never seen before. Long white and red sea worms swayed in the water like they were dancing. Some of them were as tall as me!

We traveled along the seafloor for a while. It was like being inside the most amazing aquarium I'd ever seen. We went around one of the vents and something caught my eye. At first, I thought it was another sub, but as we got closer I realized it looked more like a giant tractor. Then I saw another, and then another. There were three of them.

"What are those?" I asked.

Each machine rolled along the seafloor, kicking up sand. They went around like giant vacuums, sucking up everything in their path. They each had a long tube that climbed up into the dark abyss.

"Is this how you map the seafloor?" I asked.

"That's a complicated question," said the captain.

CHAPTER 4
The Situation

We resurfaced and climbed back onto the captain's ship. We walked along the deck, and I saw a bunch of equipment I hadn't noticed before. The machine moved massive amounts of sand and rocks along a mechanical belt. Huge hoses sprayed the materials and then dumped them back over the side. It seemed like a mining operation, but I'd never heard of mining in the ocean.

"This is a pretty amazing setup you have here," Dad said.

"Follow me," the captain said.

Dad and I followed him through a doorway and into a filthy, rundown kitchen. Mom would not have approved. We wound through room after room and finally down a long spiral staircase. Halfway down the stairs, I saw it: gold!

Containers full of the metal lined the walls. It glowed in the dimly lit room like, well, gold!

"Did all this gold come from the seafloor?" I asked, picking up a jar.

All of a sudden the captain got excited and talked very fast. "It did. And that's not all. There are metal deposits down on the bottom that would blow your mind! Out there is a fortune waiting to be had. I've mined gold all over the world, and I've never seen anything this rich." He handed me a large container full of gold nuggets. "We may very well be floating on top of the best deposit of gold in the world. And if that isn't amazing enough, there are also massive deposits of silver, copper, zinc, and other rare metals down there. It's a miner's paradise."

"That doesn't seem like a problem," I said.

"It wasn't until a few days ago that the ground started shaking and smoke started to puff from the volcano on shore. The prime minister asked me to help determine the cause."

"Do your scientists know what has caused the earthquakes?" Dad asked.

"I'll let you in on a secret, since you're Sir Robert's friends. There are no scientists. There isn't another person on this entire ship other than you and me."

"But the prime minister said you had a team of scientists working out here," I said.

"I knew that if I told him I was miner he wouldn't let me work out here," he explained. "I said I was part of a team of scientists trying to save the environment. Who'd say no to that?""

"So you're not a scientist?" I asked.

"Failed biology in high school," he said.

"And you're all alone out here? There are no other scientists?" Dad asked.

"Not a soul. It's just me and the equipment. It's the perfect operation. My mining equipment is programmed to work around the clock. There is no crew, so no one ever gets tired, and the operation never stops. This has the potential to be the most profitable mine in all the world."

"Wait, so you're saying you lied to the prime minister?" I asked.

"Technically, yes." He nodded. "But once I start sharing the profits from my mine with the island, he'll get over it."

"Have you given him any money yet?"

"Well, not exactly," he continued. "I, um . . . meant to, but I've been kind of busy."

It was clear that the captain was being dishonest.

"I still don't know what you need from me," I said. I thought it was pretty weird that he had lied to the prime minister. He didn't seem to think it was a big deal.

"I need you to get the prime minister off my back, so I can focus on mining. I don't know what's causing the earthquakes, but I can't be bothered with the problems they're having on the island."

I thought for a moment about what he'd just said. He wasn't concerned about the danger to the people on the island at all. I wanted to confront him more about the fact that he had lied to the prime minister but decided my time was better spent trying to figure out what was causing the earthquakes.

"I'm going to need a little time to figure it out," I said. "We'll have to work fast, because I have to be back at school in a few days."

He laughed. "If you can figure out a way to solve this problem in a few days, you can have all the gold I've mined so far."

"How much have you mined?"

"About two thousand ounces," he answered.

I knew gold sold for about $1,500 per ounce. I did the math in my head. It was about three million dollars in gold! "If I can figure out a way to solve this problem, I'll consider it your deposit," I said.

CHAPTER 5
The Bottom

Later that night, Dad and I took the sub back to the bottom of the sea to get a better understanding of what was going on down there. We descended without the lights on and let the sub fall into the abyss. I held my hand in front of my face and couldn't make it out at all.

It wasn't long before we started spotting the bioluminescent creatures. If I wasn't so worried about the volcano blowing the island to bits, I would have been able to enjoy the view. Unfortunately, I couldn't get the island out of my mind, so it was hard to relax and enjoy the experience.

My phone buzzed. It was Sir Robert. I answered and his face appeared on the sub's computer screen.

"Hello, Benji!" he said. "Enjoying the wonders of the seafloor?"

"Well, yeah," I answered. "It's amazing down here, but we've got a real mess on our hands."

"I'm sure you'll straighten things out soon enough," he said calmly.

"Did you know the captain is illegally mining the seafloor? He's a pretty sneaky guy."

"I knew he was mining," he began, "but I didn't know he was illegally mining. I'm not surprised, though. He's not exactly a rule follower."

"I think this might be a bit over Benji's head," Dad said. "People could be killed if the earthquakes continue or the volcano erupts."

"I understand your concerns, Mr. Franklin, but I wouldn't place Benji in a situation I didn't think he could handle," Sir Robert said. "You've had a little time to get to know the situation. Do you have any ideas yet, Benji?"

"I need to spend a little more time on the bottom and then go check out the island. I'm sure something will come to me." As impossible as it seemed, there was a part of me that knew if I focused on the problem long enough, something would come.

"Very well then. The fate of the island rests in your hands. Over and out," he said and the screen went black.

"Well, that was helpful," Dad joked.

The depth gauges showed that we were nearing the bottom, so I clicked the lights on. I noticed a few creatures scatter out of sight and retreat back to the safety of the darkness. The vents seemed to be everywhere. Some were only a few feet high, and others soared up into the darkness, and I couldn't tell where they ended. It was nicer without the captain down here with us. Everything seemed to hum like a beehive. It was all connected and alive in a way that I'd never seen before.

The hydrothermal vents were covered in life. Everything looked like it belonged, everything but the mining bots.

The area they had mined looked like the life had been sucked from it.

I closed my eyes and tried to visualize a solution, and something hit the sub like a freight train. For a moment, I thought we'd crashed into the bottom.

"Benji! Something is staring at me!" Dad yelled.

Through the window right in front of Dad was the biggest eyeball I'd ever seen. "Hold still," I said and took a picture with my camera. I know it wasn't the safest first reaction, but how often do you get to see an eyeball the size of your father's head?

I hit the booster on the sub, and we took off like a bolt. Dad cried out like a baby. The sub didn't seem to have the force it usually had. I didn't fully understand what was going on until I saw the suckers stuck to my side of the sub. We were being attacked by a giant squid!

"You have an incoming call," Saunders said.

"We have our hands full right now," I said.

"It's your school," added Saunders.

I should have ignored the call, but I put it through. Cindy's face appeared on the screen. "Why aren't you back at school yet, Benji?" she asked.

"Hello to you too, Cindy. I'm kind of in a sticky situation right now!" I shouted.

"Looks to me like you're on some kind of adventure ride. Are you on vacation at Sea World?"

"I'm in my sub being attacked by a giant squid!"

"Sure," she said, "and I'm orbiting Mars on a pink unicorn."

The squid had completely wrapped itself around the sub. I knew that they sometimes battle with whales and thought we might be gonners.

"I'm serious!" I exclaimed. "We're in my submarine, and there's a giant squid attacking us!"

The squid turned the sub over, trying to find a way to pry it open. It was a good thing Dad and I were strapped in, or we'd have been knocked out.

"You're serious! I'm stuck here at school, and you're off having the most amazing adventure ever!"

"Maybe you don't understand the meaning of the word *attacked*!" I shouted.

"I'd give anything to be attacked by a giant squid," Cindy groaned. "I did my animal report on them last quarter. Do you remember it?"

"No," I said. "But if you're such an expert on them, why don't you help me out a little?"

She looked annoyed that I didn't remember her project, and I thought she was going to hang up, but then she said, "They're creatures of the deep and live in total darkness. Try turning on every light you have. Shine some directly into its eyes if you can."

Dad reached for the emergency kit and pulled out two powerful flashlights.

He turned them both on and shined them in the giant eye on the other side of the glass. Nothing happened for a moment, and then I felt the grip on the ship slip away and the power in the engine return. As quickly as it had appeared, it vanished.

"I can't believe I'm saying this, Cindy," I said, "but I'm glad you called."

"She just saved our lives, Benji," Dad said.

"Let's not be overly dramatic," I said. "She helped, sure, but . . ."

"I think what you're trying to say is thank you, Benji," she said.

"I think she's right," Dad added.

"Thanks," I said reluctantly.

"You're welcome," she said. "I guess you're not the only genius at our school."

"Wait a minute," I said, taking a better look at Cindy on the screen. "Where are you?"

"I'm in your 'storage' closet," she said, smirking.

CHAPTER 6
Security Glitch

I should have known the second I answered the call that she was in my office because she was sitting at my desk, but I was so distracted by the giant squid I totally blanked on it. When it was clear that the squid was gone, I said, "How do you know about my storage closet?"

"I followed you the other day after you answered that call," Cindy explained. "You disappeared so quickly it didn't make sense. I knew you had to have sneaked away somewhere."

"But the only way to open that room is by hand print recognition," I explained.

"I wouldn't say the only way," she said. "But how I got in here isn't important. The important thing is that I've found your hideout, and now I'm going to tell the principal, and you'll finally get in trouble."

"I hate to break it to you, Cindy, but Mrs. Petty knows about my office. You can tell her if you like, but she'll just want to know how you got inside when I have top-of-the line security protecting it. That's breaking and entering."

"The last time I checked," Cindy replied, "the school was public property. Why should you be able to have your own office?"

"I told you already. I'm kind of like a superhero. I need a super-cool hideout."

"I'm telling," she said and hung up.

"What was that all about?" Dad asked.

"I wish I knew," I said.

"You have a secret office at school?" Just as he finished saying the words, the water vibrated and the ground shook violently. It was as if the whole seafloor had been lifted up and shaken. We didn't really feel the earthquake in the submarine as much as we saw the seafloor vibrating.

"We need to get back to the island," I said.

"Saunders, what happened?"

"It appears there was another earthquake."

"That's what I thought. Hey, why are you letting Cindy hack into my computer?" I asked.

"I tried to stop her, sir, but she's quite clever."

I hit the turbo jets, and we were back to the island in minutes. The prime minister was already there to meet us at the dock. We climbed in his jeep. Dad sat in the front, and I sat in the back. We drove into the night. The island was so dark it reminded me of the bottom of the ocean. The sky was cloudy, and there wasn't a star in the sky. The only sound was the sound of the breeze as we rolled along. I had completely lost track of time while we were in the sub. It must have been the middle of the night.

"The lights are out again?" I asked.

"We can't keep the power up and running with all the vibrations from the earthquakes. I don't even want to think about what would happen to the island if the volcano erupted."

"Maybe I should take a closer look?"

"As you wish," he said.

I'd never seen a volcano in real life before, and as we began our climb up the mountainside, I got my first glimpse. Gray smoke puffed from the top and stood out somehow against the pitch-black sky. It reminded me of the hydrothermal vents on the seafloor.

We were driving along a narrow winding road leading up to the top of the volcano when the ground started to shake. The prime minister pulled the jeep over to the side of the road, and we waited for the shaking to pass. It was pretty scary. I felt like a bug on the window of a windshield trying to hold on for dear life. My heart raced like crazy.

"We had two more big quakes just before you arrived this evening. They were bigger than the one we're having now."

While he was talking, the vibrations got worse. The jeep bounced so hard I thought it might slide right off the road.

"It's not safe to go any farther, but you get the picture, Mr. Franklins. If this volcano erupts, the town below is in terrible danger."

We drove slowly down the road that lead up to the volcano. I knew it was possible that the earthquakes and the volcano smoking were caused by something natural, but I had a feeling something else was going on.

As we drove around the island, I noticed people seemed to be outside everywhere we went, even though it was super late.

"They're afraid to sleep inside," the prime minister said, "afraid their house will collapse on them in the night. It's safer to sleep outside."

None of us said anything on the drive to the prime minister's house. Earlier I had felt excited to be staying at the home of a leader of a country, but now, all those people sleeping outside made me feel kind of guilty.

I was so tired, though, that as soon as I hit the pillow, I fell into a deep sleep and dreamed of volcanoes, earthquakes, hydrothermal vents, and giant squid. My mind kept picturing the vents. The sub's computer had recorded the temperature of the water coming out of the vents at close to 750 degrees. It was a steady flow of hot water, and I knew, even in my dream, that there was some kind of use for all that energy.

In the morning I woke to the bed vibrating like crazy. The house felt like it was being shaken by an

invisible giant. If I didn't know that the house could collapse on me any moment, it would have been kind of fun.

Dad ran rushed in and fell on the floor because it was shaking so much. "Benji, are you okay?"

"Yeah, I'm just waking up," I said.

"This is the third one this morning," he explained. "You slept through the other two."

I couldn't believe I had slept through two earthquakes!

"Also, your phone has been ringing all morning. You might want to check it." The vibrations stopped, and Dad sat at the end of the bed holding his head.

I checked to see who had called. I was hoping it was Sir Robert. I secretly wanted him to come to the island and help me out. I was feeling a little overwhelmed by all the pressure to find a solution. It wasn't Sir Robert, though. It was Cindy. She'd called three times, and the phone was ringing again.

CHAPTER 7
Zillionaire55

I almost didn't answer, but I wanted to make sure I wasn't missing anything important at school.

"Why haven't you answered your phone?" she asked.

"Good morning to you too," I said.

"It's the middle of the night here," she explained. "We're in different time zones."

"What's so important that you had to wake me up, and you're up in the middle of the night?"

"I think I know why the island is having all the earthquakes," she said. "It's that captain."

"How do you know about the captain?" I asked.

"Come on, Benji. You're supposed to be the genius, aren't you?"

I thought for a second.

Cindy had access to my office.

"My office?" I asked.

"Yep, I'm not there now, of course, but I have remote access from my house."

"How'd you do that?"

"You need to be more creative with your passwords," Cindy said. "I mean, *zillionaire* wasn't very difficult to guess. You couldn't have worked in a few capital letters or gone with something like zillionaire55? It lacks imagination."

I couldn't believe what she was saying. Did she have access to my emails, my texts, my phone?

"You can't just hack into my stuff like that!" I said.

"I admit, it wasn't very nice of me," Cindy responded. "But as you've already pointed out, I'm not always that nice. But that's not what's important right now, Benji. I did a little research on that captain. His name is Sigmund Norway."

"And?" I asked.

"He's not a sea captain," she explained. "He's also not a scientist. He's from the northern Yukon of Alaska and owns a company that drills deep into the earth to take samples for miners, so they know if there's gold in the ground before they mine."

It hit me all at once. The reason for the earthquakes and the volcano. "He's drilling into the seafloor and causing the earthquakes," I said.

"I think so," said Cindy. "He left that part out when he talked to you."

"How did you know that?" I asked.

"Thanks to the technology in your office, I have access to the cameras on your sub. He showed you the robots that are vacuuming the seafloor, but I bet he's drilling somewhere down there too."

I was furious at Cindy, but I was also thankful for her help. There was something strange about the captain all along that I just couldn't figure out.

"Is that everything?" I asked.

"Yes, school has been pretty slow. You haven't missed much."

"We really should get going before there's another quake," Dad said.

"Benji," Cindy said, "I can log out of your system if you want. I was just so amazed when you told me where you and your dad are and what you're doing. I couldn't resist."

I thought for a moment and said, "It's okay. I probably would have done the same thing if I was in your situation, and I'm going to need all the help I can get. Just don't eat all my candy!" I warned.

"I'm not making any promises," she said.

CHAPTER 8
The Drill

If someone had told me before I left on the mission that I'd be asking Cindy for help, I'd have never believed it. But if what she had said about the captain was true, it might just help me stop the earthquakes.

Dad and I rode back to the docks with the prime minister. "I think you should come with us, sir," I said to the prime minister. "I have new information about what might be causing the earthquakes."

"Let's go," he said. "I've been dying to check out your sub since the moment you gentlemen arrived."

On the way out to the captain's ship, I explained to the prime minister what Cindy had said. She even sent me a link to the captain's website. Right on the home page of the site was a picture of him operating a giant drill, giving a thumbs up.

Minutes later, we arrived at his ship and docked. The captain was on the deck checking the gold in his wash plant. He shut off the engine as we came aboard and threw a cover over the gold on the table. He didn't look very happy to see the prime minister.

"Hello, Mr. Prime Minister," he said.

"Hello, Sigmund," the prime minister said.

The captain's face went white. "How do you know my name is Sigmund?"

"We know a lot more than that," I said. "We know that you own a drilling company."

"So?"

"So," the prime minister said, "I gave you permission to map the seafloor, but I'm getting the feeling that you are up to far more than that."

"He's mining the seafloor because it's loaded with gold and other precious metals," I said.

"I planned on sharing the profits with the island," the captain said.

"Are you drilling into the seafloor?" I asked. "Because if you are, that could be the cause of the earthquakes."

"Of course not," he said.

"Think carefully," the prime minister said. "If I find out you're lying and putting the people of my island at risk, I will have you arrested."

The captain paused for a long moment and then said, "Let's head back down. There's something you should see."

We all climbed aboard my sub and made the descent to the bottom. The captain guided us to a section of the seafloor he hadn't shown us before. A massive machine rested there. It looked like an underwater skyscraper. It soared so high up into the darkness that even with my lights on full power I couldn't see the top.

"This is my drill. I've been getting so much gold on the seafloor that I decided to drill down in hopes there would be even more."

"Why didn't you stop when you started causing the earthquakes?" I asked.

"They didn't happen every time I drilled. I figured that if I kept trying I might find spots that didn't cause the earthquakes, but it's been hard to predict."

"You realize that if the volcano on the island erupts, people could be killed?" Dad said.

They kept talking, but I couldn't hear their words anymore. As I looked out at the massive drill and the hydrothermal vents puffing black material, an idea started to take shape. It swirled in my mind all at once—the hydrothermal vents, the superhot water, the power problems on the island, the gold. I didn't know how much time had passed, but after a while Dad said, "Benji, are you listening to us?" and I snapped out of my daydream.

"I have a solution to the problems," I said.

"Which problems?" the prime minister asked.

"All of them," I said.

I hopped on my computer to work out the plan. The prime minister and the captain were arguing, but I'd stopped listening. I was in the zone. I put together my materials list and started working out pricing. Dad steered the sub back to the surface.

15,000 meters of heat-resistant piping	$2,878,000
500 steel fans	$434,000
Expanded wash plant	$654,000
20 miles of high voltage electrical cable and wiring	$1,327,000
Steel platform	$2,898,000
3 barges with crews	$1,750,000
Total cost for project	$9,941,000
20% consulting fee	$1,988,200
Total Amount Due	$11,929,200

*Nonrefundable deposit: 2,000 ounces of gold

CHAPTER 9
The Plan

When we reached the surface, I had the whole plan worked out. I printed the bill and handed it to the captain.

"What's this?" he asked.

"You called me here to find a solution to your problem. I've solved it, and if the prime minister agrees, we should be able to keep you out of jail."

"He wouldn't really have me arrested," he said nervously.

"Yes, I would," the prime minister said. "You lied to the people of my island, mined the seafloor, and drilled illegally! I intend to have you arrested unless Benji can convince me otherwise."

"My plan does a few things," I said. "First, the captain agrees to stop drilling. It's the cause of the earthquakes, and once the drilling stops, hopefully the earthquakes will too." I looked at the captain.

"Agreed," he said.

"Second, we'll place heat-resistant piping over the hydrothermal vents. As the superhot water moves up through the pipe, it will turn hundreds of fans in the pipes. The energy from the turning fans and the intense heat will generate electricity on a large barge. We'll wire the electricity to the island. You'll have more electricity than you can imagine." I looked at the prime minister.

"I like the sound of that," he said.

"Third, the black material that flows out of the hydrothermal vents is loaded with gold and other valuable metals. It'll be run through a wash plant at the surface, mined safely without any drilling or vacuuming." I took a breath. "The captain will have to share the profits he makes from the metals with

the island. Of course, I'll take 20 percent as a fee."
They all looked at me in disbelief.

"You figured all this out just now when we were underwater?" the captain asked.

"I started getting the idea last night while I slept, but it fully formed at the seafloor."

"Who is paying for such an expensive project?" the prime minister asked.

"He is," I said, pointing at the captain.

He looked like he might faint. "Why am I paying for this?" he asked.

"You were the one who started the whole thing," I told him. "You're the reason for the earthquakes and the power outages. The least you can do is help fix the problem."

"I'll have to run it by my business partner," he said.

"I didn't realize you have a business partner. I thought you were out here all on your own." I asked.

"I am, but I have a partner too."

"Get your partner on the phone," the prime minister said. "And make sure he understands that if you don't do this, you're headed to jail."

"I hear you loud and clear," the captain said.

After a short phone call, the captain hung up and said, "We agree to the terms. My partner is going to work on getting the materials. Things should start arriving tomorrow."

That night, I was so excited I could hardly sleep. The next day the materials started to come, and a massive crew of construction workers and engineers arrived on the scene. They worked around the clock for almost a week straight.

Toward the end of the week we were ready to run the first test. The sun had just set, and the island was completely dark. We had removed the old power grid and replaced it with all new wiring that connected to the hydrothermal plant on the rig.

We all stood on the deck of the ship and waited for the engineer to give me the thumbs-up. When he did, I pressed a large green button in the engine room. It opened the pipe down at the mouth of the vent on the seafloor. Superhot water from the vent raced up the pipe, spinning the fans along the way. The plant buzzed with excitement. The needles on the control panels started to move. The entire rig actually vibrated as the combination of water, heat, and electricity zoomed through the system.

The dark material from the vents started to pump out into the captain's equipment. It washed the material and captured any gold or other precious metals. All the extra sand and rocks were simply pumped over the side to fall back to the bottom of the sea.

After a few minutes the system was at full power. The lights from the houses and streetlights on the island blinked a few times and then came on for good. I thought the prime minister was going to cry.

He hugged the captain and everyone cheered.

It was a pretty amazing feeling. I was so happy to help the island and save it from the earthquakes that would have continued if we hadn't stopped the captain from drilling. The whole atmosphere on the ship felt like one big party.

CHAPTER 10
Homeward

The prime minister and the people on the island were thrilled. We'd managed to stop the earthquakes and settle the volcano. As a bonus, the new system provided free electrical power to the island. As a double bonus, the power plant was also a precious metal mine! The island was in way better shape than when we arrived.

The next day they had a big festival to celebrate the end of the earthquakes and the beginning of a safe future. The prime minister invited Dad and me as guests of honor, but it was time to head home. We'd been gone for far too long. Mom was getting worried, and Mrs. Petty wasn't very happy about how much school I'd missed.

On the flight home I got a call from Sir Robert. "Hello, Benji," he said. "Where are you?"

"I wondered the same thing about you," I said.

"What do you mean, lad?" he asked.

"I mean that you sent Dad and me to the middle of the Atlantic to handle the biggest challenge of my life, and then you went on vacation."

"I knew you'd be able to handle the task," he said. "And even though I was on holiday, I knew what was going on with you the whole time."

"How? Did you hack into my computers too?"

"Of course not. Sigmund kept me up to date every step of the way."

"He did? I don't understand."

"We're partners. He is very good at the mechanical aspects of things, but he doesn't do a thing involving money unless he checks with me first. This solution of yours cost me a pretty penny."

I found it a little suspicious that Sir Robert would be mixed up with someone as dishonest as the captain, and that he'd keep it from me. I would have thought he would have told me earlier. It made me wonder what else he wasn't telling me. I said goodbye and shut off my phone. I needed a break from everything. It felt good to be headed home.

I was still thinking about Sir Robert as Dad and I reentered the atmosphere about an hour later. I was glad he had faith in me to solve the problem on my own, but I couldn't help wondering if he knew what the captain was up to the whole time and simply sent me there to clean up the mess.

We cruised to the harbor near our house and dropped the sub. The same people we'd waved to on the way out were there again. I wondered if they'd been so shocked the first time they saw me in my spaceship that they were frozen there and hadn't left.

We flew to the farm where Mom waited.

We landed in the hangar. It felt so good to be home. Mom gave me a big hug and a kiss when I got out of the spaceship. "I can't believe you've been gone so long!" she said.

"I know," Dad said. "It was a long trip. You would have been proud of your son."

"I'm always proud of him," she said, pinching my cheeks.

"He saved an entire island. Thanks to him, they don't have to worry about earthquakes or how they're going to power their island anymore."

Mom and Dad talked some more while I unloaded our luggage. Then I started unloading the gold. The captain had given me the two thousand ounces as part of my payment, as we agreed. It was so much gold I couldn't believe it.

"What is that?" Mom said as I hauled the massive amounts of gold from the ship.

"It's the gold from the mission. I have two thousand ounces here," I said. "I figured we could sell it and put the money toward your farm."

Mom looked like her jaw might hit the floor. "Benji Franklin, you are an amazing boy. I might just start stitching you a cape," she said.

"A cape?" I asked.

"A lot of superheroes wear them," she said, giving me a hug.

I didn't think I was ready for a cape yet, but I had a feeling the idea might grow on me.

INVOICE NO: 1004990698

NOTICE OF PAYMENT

FROM: BENJI FRANKLIN
TO: CAPTAIN SIGMUND NORWAY

15,000 meters of heat-resistant piping	$2,878,000
500 steel fans	$434,000
Expanded wash plant	$654,000
20 miles of high voltage electrical cable and wiring	$1,327,000
Steel platform	$2,898,000
3 barges with crews	$1,750,000
Total cost for project	$9,941,000
20% consulting fee	$1,988,200
Total Amount Due	$11,929,200

PAID!

*Nonrefundable deposit: 2,000 ounces of gold

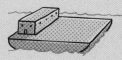

PAYMENT DUE UPON RECEIPT

Part Two

CHAPTER 11
Three Billion Is Bonkers

Dad and I were out in the shop working on a robot he'd designed. It was a pretty cool idea, and he'd put a ton of time into it. As the robot moved, it created friction. The friction was used to create electricity, and the electricity was then used to continue powering the robot. You didn't have to plug it in or use batteries. It just went on its own. He'd built it out of parts from an old computer, a metal garbage can, and a pair of Rollerblades.

I was so focused on the robot that I hardly noticed the sound of a helicopter landing in the field behind the shop. I might not have even noticed it at all if it weren't for all the dust it kicked up. Dust swirled through the doorway like a sandstorm. I was glad I was wearing a welding mask

Dad and I walked out of the shop without a

word and looked at the copter coming to rest in the field. A year ago, I would have been shocked to see a helicopter landing on our property, but my life had become pretty exciting lately. I wasn't really that surprised.

The blades slowed and three men got out. One wore a fancy business suit and the other two wore all black. They all had on black sunglasses and looked like they were in the Secret Service or something.

The two guys stayed close to the other guy as he walked toward Dad and me. It was like a scene out of an action movie, but if it were an action movie, he would have walked in slow motion.

The blades on the copter had completely stopped by the time he reached us.

"I'm looking for Benji Franklin," he said, taking off his glasses.

"I had a feeling you'd say that," my dad said, pulling off his welding mask.

"I'm Benji Franklin," I said, leaving mine on.

"I can't believe you're really a kid," he said. He was pretty short, much shorter than Dad. He had a long white beard that didn't seem to match the fancy suit.

"I had a feeling you'd say that too," Dad said.

"Is there somewhere we can talk that's more private?" he asked.

I looked around. There wasn't another soul in

sight. The only other people were his two partners.

"Don't you trust your buddies over there?" I asked.

"I don't know who to trust these days," he said.

Dad waved for him to follow and walked back toward the workshop. The workshop and my house sit on property that has been in our family for generations. Most people would take one look at it and think it was a junkyard, but to me it was like buried treasure. Old car parts, pieces of boats and airplanes, and mysterious pieces of large equipment poked out from long, overgrown grass.

There were half-finished projects all over the workshop. Dad and I had been working, so it was even more of a mess than usual. I could tell Dad was trying to find something clean for the man to sit on but couldn't.

"I won't take too much of your time. My name is Mark Crow," the man said, clearly realizing there was nowhere for him to sit in his fancy suit. "I have a problem that I'd like solved as quietly as possible, and I'm told Benji might be the right person for the job."

I sat on one of the boxes a delivery guy had brought in earlier that morning. Mr. Crow sat on the one next to me. As I got comfortable, I realized I didn't know what was in the boxes, but they had been sent from my school. They were pretty big. It made me wonder what was inside.

"What's the problem?" I asked.

"Benji just finished a job," Dad said before Mr. Crow could reply. "He has a tremendous amount of schoolwork to complete, and I don't know that he'll have the time for anything outside of his studies."

I shook my head to indicate that I disagreed. Although I had just returned from a job, I was ready to get back to work.

"What's the problem?" I asked Mr. Crow again.

"It's kind of complicated," he said.

"Complicated is kind of my thing."

"I represent a very small but powerful group of business people," he explained. "Recently we've all been the victims of the same crime."

"What kind of crime?" I asked.

I was feeling more like a superhero than ever. I imaginged my dad as my loyal sidekick. He's a little old for a sidekick, but what can you do?

"Benji is more of a scientist than a detective," Dad said.

"I've been known to dabble in a little detective work from time to time," I said, embracing my inner superhero.

"A robbery," he said, glancing over his shoulder.

"Where'd the robbery take place?" I asked. "Also, you do know there's no one out here watching us, right?"

"You can never be too safe. And to answer your question about the location of the robbery, that's the complicated part. It wasn't one robbery. It was many large robberies that happened all at once. They're probably taking place right now."

"I don't get it," Dad said.

"We own some of the largest companies in the world. We own fast food chains, clothing companies, sporting goods stores, credit cards companies, car companies—you name it, and we probably own it," he said.

"Burger Slam?" I asked.

"We own it."

"Game Revolution?" I asked.

"We own that too, and most of the companies that make the games they sell."

"Jumbo's Food Mart?" I asked.

"Own it and most of the companies that supply the groceries for the stores. Like I said, if you've heard of it, one of us probably owns it. If you haven't heard of it, we probably own it. That's what makes what's happened so unbelievable."

"I still don't really understand," I said.

"Our digital transactions, when someone uses a credit card, are being hijacked."

"When you say hijacked . . . ?" Dad asked.

"I mean that the charges are going through— customers are paying by using their credit cards—

but the money doesn't go into our accounts. It disappears," said Mr. Crow.

"How much money did you lose?" I asked.

"So far, about three billion."

"You mean million?" I asked.

"No, you heard me correctly. We've lost about three billion dollars," he groaned.

If I had long hair, it would have blown back. "Billion with a 'b' like the word bonkers?" I asked.

"Billion with a 'b' like bananas," he said.

"WOW! That's, well . . . berserk!" I joked.

"No kidding. It's a bit of a nightmare to be honest. We're not sure what to do. We can't stop taking credit cards or our customers will think something is wrong."

"But something is wrong," I pointed out.

"Yes, but they can't know that. We have to conduct business as usual, but we're losing a ton of money in the process."

"You should really talk with the police or the FBI," Dad pointed out.

"We would like to keep this as quiet as possible. If we involve law enforcement, the story be all over the news, and people might stop using our stores. We want this fixed quickly and quietly. We can't have people thinking our stores aren't safe to shop in."

"But they're not safe to shop in," I said.

"That's why I'm here talking to you. I need that fixed, and I need it fixed as quickly as possible."

"I'll have to talk with Benji's mother and his school about this before he can commit to helping you," Dad said.

"I completely understand, but we'll need to know in the next twenty-four hours. Every second that passes could be more money lost. Also, if news of this spreads, we'll have a major panic on our hands. So you can't tell anyone."

CHAPTER 12

Merci

"There's no way you can take on another job," Mom said that night at dinner.

"I know I've been super busy lately," I pleaded, "but this is an amazing mission."

"You mean 'job,' Benji. You get so caught up in them that they really become full-time jobs."

"Remember, he likes to think of himself as a superhero. So he prefers it if we call them missions," Dad said.

I nodded. He was right. I'd gone from being a kid that invented a successful app to a guy that secretly solved the world's problems. Why shouldn't they be called missions? Calling them jobs sounded so chore-like that it just didn't feel right.

"How about we call them adventures?" Dad suggested.

"It really doesn't matter what we call them," Mom said. "Benji needs to take a break for a while."

"Sir Robert thinks I should stop going to school for a while and focus on my missions and creating new apps," I explained.

Sir Robert had said it more than once, and I knew he'd mentioned it to Mom and Dad.

"Sir Robert is not your mother," said Mom.

"He is a billionaire who's traveled the world." I said, knowing I was pushing it with my mom.

"And as much as he's helped you, I'm beginning to wonder if he has your best interests in mind. But we're not talking about him right now. We're talking about you, and you need to experience a regular childhood and a regular education."

"But Benji has a rocket ship, a submarine, and more money than we can keep track of," Dad added.

"I think the whole 'regular childhood' thing might be a stretch at this point."

"I realize that," Mom said, "but I want him to have as regular a childhood as he can. I accept that you're already wildly successful at a very young age, but that doesn't mean you should stop learning and stop living like a regular kid."

"You always say to use my knowledge for the greater good, right?" I asked.

"Yes," she said.

"Well, this man that stopped by today said there are thousands of people who have been robbed. They need my help."

"That sounds like a job for the police."

"He wants it done quietly," Dad interrupted.

"Isn't there anyone else who can solve these problems? How come all these successful people are always coming to you to save the day?" Mom asked.

"You know the answer to that question," I said.

"A superhero, huh?" she asked giving a slight smile.

"I'm not like the rest of the kids, Mom."

"I realized that when you taught yourself French in kindergarten," she said.

"It does sound like an interesting opportunity," Dad added. Dad was funny. I could tell he was just as excited or even more than me, but he tried not to show it in front of Mom.

"If you can figure out a way to solve this," she paused, "mission, without missing any school, I'll give you my permission."

"*Merci*," I said.

"You're welcome," she said, giving me a smile. "School comes first."

"Agreed," I said.

Of course, I had no idea how I was going to solve the heist without missing any school. School was very demanding, and I'd missed a lot of it lately.

I knew I had a bunch of assignments piling up, but I didn't know what was due and when. I'd have to get my nose back in the books and get caught up if Mom was ever going to let me work on the mission.

CHAPTER 13
I Get Your Point, But I Don't Like It

In the morning, my car picked me up earlier than usual. It was my first day back after my last mission, and I wanted to get on top of things.

"How was your last mission, sir?" Mr. Kensington, my driver, asked.

"It was a total adventure," I said. "I got to use my submarine, and I was attacked by a giant squid. It was pretty awesome."

"A giant squid! Wow! You're leading an exciting life these days," he said. "Were you paid well?"

"A few million dollars, and I'm part owner in a deep sea gold mine."

"Not bad for a week's work," Kensington said.

"Not bad at all!" I agreed.

He stopped in front of the school. "Let's hope your good luck holds up when you meet with your principal." I thanked him and walked into the school. I went straight to the principal's office.

She was on the phone, but hung up when she saw me coming. "Benji Franklin," she said, "how nice of you to stop by and say hello."

The tone in her voice sounded kind of like she was upset with me, which was strange because she was usually very cool.

"Is something wrong?" I asked.

"No, but you've missed more school than I had expected on your last adventure. I spoke with your mother about it, and we agree that you should take a break from missing school for a while."

"I know," I said. "We already talked about it at home." I realized there was no point in trying to get out of more school or make a pitch as to why I needed a few more days to work on the new mission. "I think you're probably right," I said.

"Good. You're going to need all of your attention on schoolwork in order to catch up on the assignments you've missed."

I figured I'd missed a few assignments, but it couldn't be too bad. She logged onto her computer and made a face. "Oh my. You have several assignments that are overdue."

"That can't be right. You said you were going to send me any assignments to complete while I was away. No one sent me anything to work on."

"I had asked Cindy to keep track of your assignments and pass them on to you since she's in all your classes," the principal explained.

"She didn't email me anything while I was away," I said. It figured too, because Cindy was always giving me a hard time about everything. She probably didn't send them on purpose just so I'd get in trouble.

"That's odd. Why don't you track her down and see if she'll catch you up on what you've missed."

I wasn't looking forward to seeing Cindy. She always gave me such a hard time about being out of school. She did help me a little bit with the mission, which was a nice surprise, but now it seemed like we were right back to her giving me a hard time.

I walked out of Mrs. Petty's office and down to my secret office in the storage closet. I held my hand up to the word *storage* on the door and it unlocked. I glanced over my shoulder to make sure no one was looking and slipped in.

I knew Cindy had been in my office while I was away, but I still couldn't figure out how she did it. The only way to get in was to scan your hand over the sign, and as far as I knew, I was the only one with the same fingerprints as me.

I sat at my desk and realized right away that my computer and all my screens were gone. An ancient-looking computer, like the ones in the classrooms, sat on the desk. I felt like I was in some kind of a time warp. I hadn't used a computer that old since I was a baby. The computer was probably older than me! I tried to log in, but it denied me access.

Just then I heard the door open and close. From behind the pile of boxes in front of my desk, Cindy appeared. "Welcome back," she said.

"How'd you get in here? Where's my computer?" I asked.

"Didn't your mother ever teach you to say hello to someone when they say hello to you?"

"Of course she did," I said, "but right now I would like to know where my computers went."

"Mrs. Petty gave me permission to remove them. We had them sent back to your house."

That must have been the boxes that were delivered the day before. "Why would she do that?"

"She realized, after I pointed it out, that it wasn't fair for you to have access to the latest technology when the rest of the students use the oldest computers known to humans."

"But she agreed to let me use this office," I said.

"That's true, and I tried to convince her that it was unfair and you should lose that privilege, but she said she had worked out some sort of agreement with you and that man Sir Robert."

She was right. Sir Robert had convinced Mrs. Petty that if my parents were going to make me continue to go to school like a regular kid, I should have a secret office where I could work on my missions in quiet. Mrs. Petty agreed. Now Cindy was trying to take that away.

"What do you care if I have a secret office?"

"Because it's not fair. I'm the head of the Committee for Fairness and Equality for our school, and I couldn't sit by while something like this was going on that is unfair for all the students."

"But how am I supposed to get anything done in here?" I asked. "These computers look like they came over on the Mayflower."

"Don't be ridiculous," she said. "There weren't computers when the Mayflower sailed."

I didn't have time to explain to Cindy that I was only kidding because the first bell rang.

"We'll have to find some time later today to talk about all the assignments you have due," she said.

"How come you didn't send me my assignments? I could have worked on them while I was away."

"I tried emailing you on the computers from school, but the connection is very unreliable. Most of the time the emails don't go through."

"Why didn't you just send it from your home computer or tell me when we talked on the phone?"

"Mrs. Petty asked me to email you the assignments from school. That's what I did. I tried from school several times, and the technology failed. That's not my fault," Cindy said.

I didn't want to spend another moment arguing with Cindy, so I slipped out into the hall and made my way to my first class.

As soon as I walked in the door, my math teacher handed me a folder full of work that was due by the end of the week. The same thing happened in reading, writing, social studies, and science.

I stopped into Mrs. Petty's office at the end of the day, plopped all the work on her desk, and fell into the chair. She looked at me and smiled. It was kind of weird, because I didn't feel like smiling at all, and she had a huge grin on her face.

"It looks like you have some work ahead of you this week," she said.

"I do, and I'll get it done," I explained. "But I don't understand why Cindy or my teachers couldn't have emailed everything I needed."

"The system isn't very reliable when it comes to emails and the Internet," said Mrs. Petty. "Cindy tried, but her emails must not have gone through."

"Don't you think that's kind of a problem?" I asked. "Everything takes place online these days. The school should really have better computers."

"You're right, but our system is very outddated."

"What about my office? How come Cindy snuck in and removed all of my technology?"

"Don't ask me how she got in. I don't even have access to that space, and I'm the principal. However, it did seem like the only fair thing to do. You can use the office,

of course, as we agreed. But I feel it's not fair to the other students if you're allowed access to the better equipment."

"But those were my computers," I reminded her. "I paid for them. I wasn't using up any of the school's resources."

"True," Mrs. Petty agreed. "But unless you plan on buying new computers for the entire school, I'm afraid you'll have to use the same old computers as everyone else when you're in school."

I could buy new computers for everyone in the district if I wanted to, but it wasn't my job to supply computers for the district.

"As much as I'd like to help the school," I said, "It's not fair for me to buy them for everyone."

"Then you'll understand how it's not fair for you to have the best of the best while the rest of the kids have to work with the old computers."

I understood her point, but I still didn't like it.

CHAPTER 14
Name Your Price

That night, Mom, Dad, and I were at the farm checking up on the livestock when Mr. Crow landed his helicopter on one of the old runways. The farm had been an old airport before we converted it to a farm.

The same two Secret Service–looking guys from the other day were with him. He introduced himself to Mom and invited us all to go for a ride. He said he wanted to show us something that might help us make our decision. I didn't tell him that Mom had already decided to give me permission to take his mission.

"It's happened again," he said over the headphones once we were in the air.

"What's happened exactly?" Mom asked.

"The majority of all the money that exchanged hands today across the entire country for my group's businesses has vanished. One moment it was there and the next—POOF—it was all gone. We're talking about almost every transaction from our stores, websites, doctor's offices, and hospitals. It's a major situation, and we can't keep it quiet much longer. And when word gets out about this, we're all in big trouble. Worse, if our businesses suffer, the people that work in them might lose their jobs."

"Can't you simply track the money?" Dad asked.

"We're talking about electronic money, Mr. Franklin," Mr. Crow explained. "It's not like bills that we can put fingerprint powder on or track the numbers on the bills or something like that. This money is digital. It went somewhere in cyberspace, but we don't know where 'somewhere' is."

My phone vibrated. It was Sir Robert.

"Please do not breathe a word of this to anyone else," Mr. Crow warned.

"It's just Sir Robert. He's basically my partner," I said.

"No disrespect, but I don't want Robert knowing about what's happened," he said.

"You know Sir Robert?" I asked.

"Yes," Mr. Crow replied, "and I don't want him to know what's happened or that you're helping me. He's one of my competitors. I don't want him to have the satisfaction of knowing I'm being hacked. For all I know, it's him."

"Please put your phone away, Mr. Franklin," one of the guys in black said.

I clicked to ignore the call and felt kind of funny about it. Sir Robert had always been my mentor and someone I talked to about all of my missions. It would be strange working without his help.

"I realize that Sir Robert and you have a strong

history, but if you're to take this job, you mustn't breathe a word of the details to him. Do you think you can do that?"

I looked at Mom and Dad. "I can." I was really excited about the mission, but I didn't expect to have to hide it from Sir Robert.

I felt myself slip off into a bit of a daydream. There were so many things on my mind—the schoolwork I'd missed, the missing money, Sir Robert. It all swirled in my head.

"Do you have any ideas on how to figure out what's going on?" Mom asked. She knew me so well. Sometimes I slip into a bit of a haze, and then the idea comes to me. It's kind of like a waking dream.

"I do," I said. I had the beginnings of a plan forming.

"Your reputation for working fast is accurate," Mr. Crow said.

"It's not fully formed yet," I explained, "but I can see a solution to your problem. I think we can catch the hacker and get your businesses back to normal, but it's not going to be cheap."

This was always one of my favorite parts of the mission. It was interesting to see how people would react to the news that solving their problem might be fast but very expensive.

"If you can solve this problem, you can name your price," he said. That was the answer I'd been hoping for.

"Fantastic," I said. "Do you have any companies that sell computers?"

"Of course," Mr. Crow replied. "We own the three biggest computer companies in the country."

"I'm going to need a lot of computers," I said.

"How many?" he asked.

"About five hundred to start, but I'll need way more when the job is done."

"That doesn't seem like a problem," he said.

"I'll need you to deliver them to my school first thing tomorrow morning."

"I'll make the call the moment we're back on the ground," he said.

CHAPTER 15
Special Delivery

I woke up before the sun rose the next morning. I was super excited to get to work. I looked out my window and saw that the light in the shop was already on, so I got dressed and went down.

"What are you doing up already?" Dad asked.

"I guess I'm excited to get to work." I couldn't wait to see Mrs. Petty's face when those computers started rolling in. "What are you doing up so early?"

"I had a breakthrough on my robot last night. I haven't been to bed yet," Dad said. Dad sometimes got so caught up in his work that he worked through the night.

I felt my phone buzz in my pocket. It was Sir Robert calling. "I should answer this," I said.

"Hello, old boy," Sir Robert said. His face was crowded in close to the screen on his phone.

"Hi, Sir Robert."

"How are you, Benji? I haven't heard from you since you returned from your last journey."

"I know," I said. "I've been busy getting back to my schoolwork. I have a pile to get to that's pretty massive."

"Tell your principal you're busy with things far more important than reports and homework. The world is your classroom now."

"Tell that to my mom," I said. "She doesn't even want me taking on any new missions."

"She wants you to be like other kids. I get that. I just don't feel school should be holding you back from your calling in life. Have you had any job offers since your last mission? Several of my business associates have asked for your contact information. You're services are very much in demand."

"Nothing too exciting. Like I said, Mom won't let me take off any more time from school, so I can't do much." I felt bad about not telling him the truth, but I didn't know if I could completely trust him.

Later that day during second period, I noticed three massive black trucks roll up in front of the school. Through the window I watched as one of the drivers walked up the front path and went in the school. I waited for the announcement that I was

sure was going to come over the PA system once Mrs. Petty learned what was in the trucks.

I looked at the clock. The announcement would come any second. I counted down in my mind. Five, four, three, two, one . . . It came right on cue: "Excuse the interruption. Would Benji Franklin report to the main office, please? Benji Franklin to the main office."

The kids in the class all looked at me like I was in trouble, but I just smiled. I couldn't wait to see the look on Mrs. Petty's face. I strolled out of class and made my way slowly to the office.

I walked in and Mrs. Petty said, "May I speak with you in my office, please, Mr. Franklin?"

"Of course," I said. The driver sat in the chair that kids sit in when they're in trouble and waiting for the principal.

We walked in, and she closed the door behind us.

"What's going on?" she asked once the door was completely closed.

"You said I could have my computers back if I updated the computers for the school. I figured out a way to make that happen," I explained.

"Benji, as generous and considerate as that may be, you can't simply make a decision like this without asking me first."

"I thought we talked about it yesterday," I said.

"Well, I didn't expect you to go out and find a way to provide new computers to the entire school the next day," Mrs. Petty replied.

"Well, I did," I said. "It's kind of how I roll.

"It's not that simple, Benji," she said. "We are one school in a very large school district. I can't provide new computers to this school if the other schools don't have the same opportunities."

I knew she would say that and had already set it up with Mr. Crow so that I could get more computers if I needed them.

"If you allow me to install these computers today, I promise you that I'll get new computers for the entire school district when my mission is over," I said. Then I realized I was in a position to negotiate. "But I'd like something in return."

"I'm listening," she said.

"Give me a week off, but in the school. All my attention is going to have to be on my new mission. I can't be distracted by reports, late homework, and going to class. I also need you to forgive my missed assignments."

"This is highly irregular. Students don't generally come into the principal's office and negotiate their way out of missed assignments and going to class."

"But they also don't offer to supply new computers for the school district. I'm saving you millions and helping the school at the same time."

"You have a good point," she said. "I'll give you a week to complete your new mission. If at the end of the week you supply new computers for the entire district, I'll direct your teachers to forgive your assignments."

"You have yourself a deal," I said. "You also have new computers for the school."

"I've never experienced a student quite like you, Benji Franklin," said Mrs. Petty.

I wasn't sure if she meant that as a compliment or if she was criticizing me, but I had an opportunity to solve the heist, avoid my missing work, and keep my promise to Mom that I wouldn't miss any time from school.

"One more thing," I said.

"I'm afraid to ask," she said.

Then I said something that I thought might just knock her clear out of her chair. "I'd like to partner with Cindy on this mission."

CHAPTER 16
Invisible Data

Later that night, Dad and I decided we should head up into space. We needed to get a better look at the satellites orbiting the planet to have a better understanding of how they worked. We climbed into the cockpit, and my ship's computer said, "Good evening, Mr. Franklin and Mr. Franklin."

"Good evening, Saunders," I said.

Saunders opened the roof of the building. The stars shined about as bright as could be. We lifted off slow, rising up like a helicopter, hovering above the hangar. Once we were high enough and had cleared the building, I hit the booster rockets, and we were off like a bolt. Within minutes, we were out of Earth's atmosphere.

I turned on the GPS and asked Saunders to show us all the satellites in orbit. Then I asked Saunders to show me all the satellites owned by Mr. Crow's companies.

Saunders was a robot, I understood that, but I kind of thought of him as a person too. He seemed so human that it was hard to remember that he was simply a complex computer program.

"I'm displaying all the known satellites orbiting Earth in blue. I've highlighted the ones owned by the Crow Corporation and its companies in green.

"Thank you," I said.

"You do not have to thank me, sir," Saunders said.

"It's just a computer," Dad said.

"Yes, but he's extraordinarily smart." As I said the words, I felt something about the mission click into place. The transactions were done by computers. People slid their credit cards through the computers at the store and after that every other step was completed by a computer.

The reason why Mr. Crow and his companies couldn't figure out who was stealing their money was because the person stealing their money wasn't a person at all. It was probably a computer programmed to steal and then cover its tracks.

Luckily for me, I just had five hundred new computers installed at school. All I had to do now was program them to work together, and we might be able to catch the thief.

"Benji, are you okay?" Dad asked. "You haven't said anything in a while."

I had slipped off into a daydream. It felt like only a few seconds had passed. "I'm fine," I said. "Just thinking."

"We're approaching the first satellite," he said.

I looked out the window of the spaceship. The satellite was like a floating tube with mirrors and

long, flat panels on either side. The panels were solar panels and tilted toward the sun for power.

We zoomed ahead to the next satellite. It looked a lot like the first one, but it was much larger. The most interesting thing about seeing the satellites up close in space was that you couldn't see the data. It's completely invisible. Dad and I zipped from satellite to satellite. If you didn't know each one was transmitting loads of data back and forth to Earth, you'd think it was just a floating piece of metal.

There had to be a way to follow the data and track where it went and how it moved. For that, I realized, I'd need a few satellites of my own.

Dad and I had made and launched satellites ourselves in the past. We even have one that orbits Earth looking for dangerous asteroids. The ones we've made, though, were not nearly as advanced as what I needed for this mission. I needed a few satellites that could work faster than the satellites being robbed. And I needed them right away.

CHAPTER 17

Welcome To My Lair

That night I called Mr. Crow while we were in space and told him we'd need a few satellites immediately in order to solve the problem.

"Benji," Mr. Crow began, "I can honestly say that when I was put in touch with you I didn't really have high hopes that you'd be able to actually find a solution to my problem. I didn't think a child was capable of tackling something so enormous, but people told me to trust that you were capable of the task, and I did. Who knew there were twelve-year-olds with their own spaceships?"

"Actually, I'm the only one," I said.

"Of course you are," he said. "I will get you the satellite you need, but I'd also like to meet tomorrow morning to talk about your plan. Can you put together a price list for me so I have an idea of what I'm going to spend? I'll have to run it by my partners."

"I'll be at school tomorrow," I said. "But if you'd like to stop by, I'll be working on your mission. I'll send over exactly what I'll need and a price breakdown in a few minutes."

"I'll see you tomorrow then," said Mr. Crow. "Right now, I'm going to get to work on finding you those satellites. See you in the morning."

I typed out the bill for Mr. Crow and emailed it to him.

Fuel for spaceship	$175,000
Satellite delivery	$200,000
Total cost for project	$4,175,000
20% Consulting fee	$200,000
Total amount due	$4,375,000

*2,000 computers No charge, supplied by Mr. Crow (Value $2,200,000)
*Satellite Supplied by Mr. Crow (Value $1,600,000)

The next morning, I had Kensington pick me up at four o'clock.

"You're really getting a lot of schoolwork done," he said. "I don't think I've ever seen you this committed to school."

"I made a deal with my mom and the principal. I agreed to not miss any school, and I agreed to solve the mission by the end of the week."

"It sounds like a lot of pressure," he said.

I guess it was, but I didn't think of it that way. To me it was an adventure and a game all rolled up into one. I'd managed to convince Mom to let me take the mission, and I'd convinced the principal to let me skip class all week. I had to succeed.

I was at school before Mrs. Petty. I put a note on her desk to call me when she arrived and went to my office to work.

I tried to hack my way into one of Mr. Crow's satellites, but it was too complex. Then I tried to access the computers at a few of his stores, but the code was too complicated to crack. I knew if I had more time I'd be able to get in without a problem, but we didn't have time. I'd have to figure something out—and fast.

Before I knew it, my phone rang, and it was seven thirty. It was Mrs. Petty. "Good morning, Benji," she said. "I just got in and saw your note. Also, there's a man named Mr. Crow and two other gentlemen here to meet with you."

"Super! Can you all come down to my office?"

A few minutes later they knocked on the door. I let them in and closed the door behind them. I had set up my computers already and was busy at work.

"What is this?" Mr. Crow asked.

"Good morning, Mr. Crow. This is my lair."

"I should have figured you'd have a lair," he said. "A secret hide out, stopping the bad guys—all you need is a cape and you're all set."

"You're not the first person to tell me that," I said. "I've been thinking about wearing a cape, but I think that might be going a little overboard."

"Just a little," Cindy said, walking in.

I didn't know how she'd made it in again! I'd closed the door behind Mrs. Petty and Mr. Crow. She had figured out a way to hack my security and instead of being mad about it, I was kind of curious.

"How do you do it?" I asked.

"I told you," replied Cindy, "you're not the only genius in our school."

CHAPTER 18

It's All About You

Cindy looked like she woke up on the wrong side of the cage or something. I decided it was probably the wrong time to ask her more questions about how she was getting through my security.

"I know that you and I haven't exactly gotten along in the past," I said.

"You can say that," she said.

"But I have a new mission, and I think you can be a big help."

"Why would you want my help?" Cindy asked.

"Well," I began, "you're always giving me a hard time about missing school when I'm on my missions. I thought that if you helped me with one, you might understand how important they are and get off my back."

"So it's all about you? Why am I not surprised?"

"Actually," Mrs. Petty said. "Benji's missions are usually about helping other people. If they weren't, I would never let him miss school. In this case, the people he's helping are the students of our school."

"Can I tell her what's going on?" I asked Mr. Crow.

"If you think she needs to know," he said.

I explained to Cindy that Mr. Crow's companies were being robbed and that I had a plan to stop it, but I needed her help.

"Why do you need my help?" she asked.

"You're the head of every committee in this school. You're used to working with large groups of people to get something done.

"I still don't understand why you need my help," she said.

"I'm launching a few satellites today that are going to capture all the digital activity at Mr. Crow's businesses. I've written a program that captures the data and slows it down, but the program is too long and complicated for me to enter it on my own. I don't have time to enter the computer code by the end of the week. Also, I think that whoever is doing the hacking on Mr. Crow's system has coded the computers so other computers can't detect what's going on. To catch this cyber criminal we're going to need eyes on the data, not just computers. This project is going to take the whole school. We'll need every student working."

Mrs. Petty leaned back in her chair and made a strange face, like she was in pain. I thought she must make the same face when she's in the dentist's chair.

"You can guarantee new computers for the entire district?" she asked.

"Guaranteed," I said, looking at Mr. Crow. He nodded.

"I'll have to meet with the teaching staff and see if they agree to this," said Mrs. Petty.

"Think of it as a team-building exercise. If we can work together as a team, we can learn so many skills we'll need in the real world," Cindy said.

"We never discussed this," Mrs. Petty said. "The school gives the student assignments, Benji. It's generally not the other way around."

Mrs. Petty was quiet for a few minutes, and then she said, "What do you think, Cindy? Can you put together a committee to write the computer code for Mr. Crow?"

"I can. And I will under one condition," she said. "I don't take orders from you. I'm in charge of the kids."

"This is all highly unusual," Mr. Crow said. "My partners are never going to believe I'm letting a bunch of school kids solve a multibillion dollar cyber heist. I'll give you until the end of the week, Benji."

"Are you in?" I asked Cindy.

"I'm in," she replied. "Let's get to work."

***

Mrs. Petty called a meeting with all the teachers to explain that for the next few days the kids in the school would be working on a school-wide computer project.

Cindy got to work breaking up my code into assignments for small groups. Each group would be assigned a part of the code to enter in the computer.

At nine o'clock, Mrs. Petty announced that we were having an assembly. The entire school stopped working and went to the auditorium. Cindy and I joined Mrs. Petty on the stage.

"Good morning, students," she said. "I've called you together to share some very exciting news. As you all know by now, Benji Franklin is often out of school because he has been working on top-secret missions. This week, you will all get a chance to be involved in one."

The room was quiet. The kids didn't seem to know what was going on. Mrs. Petty waved me over to the microphone. I'd never talked to a large group like that before and felt really nervous all of the sudden. I leaned in to the microphone, which I could hardly reach.

"Good morning. I know a lot of you secretly hate that I get to miss school a lot because of my super-cool missions, but this week you guys get a chance to be a part of one." The room was still quiet, and I couldn't tell what the kids were thinking. I knew I had to turn up the interest level if I was going to win them over. "Mrs. Petty has agreed to cancel classes and homework for the rest of the week!" I announced.

The room erupted. Kids acted as if they'd won the lottery or something.

Mrs. Petty made her way back to the microphone, and the room quieted. "We're going to work together on a school-wide computer-programming project," she explained. "While we're working on the project, I have canceled classes and homework. Cindy Myers will divide the school into one hundred groups of ten. Each group will be responsible for entering a string of code that will be part of the larger code that will help Benji complete his mission."

The room cheered again, and then Cindy took the microphone. "I'll email every student his or her group and the string of code to enter. Benji and I will be around if you need any help. We have only a few days to do this, so please work together and do your best. If we can complete the project successfully, we can earn computers for the whole school district."

CHAPTER 19

Invisible Money

The next day, Mr. Crow sent me the access codes and passwords to all of his satellites. Cindy and I helped each group at school to start working on writing code and linking everything into the new satellite. It was a massive job, but by breaking it into smaller pieces it didn't seem impossible. Cindy was really good about making the groups and keeping them on track.

After school, I was in my room waiting for Mr. Kensington to pick me up and drive me to the farm so Dad and I could launch the satellites. There was a knock at the door, and Mom walked in.

"Benji, I got emails from a few of the moms from your school today," Mom began. "When I told you that you had to stay in school if you wanted to work on the mission for Mr. Crow, I didn't expect you to shut down classes and put the entire school to work."

"I didn't either," I said. "But it's how things worked out. If we can pull it off, Mr. Crow will give new computers to the entire school district."

"I don't know how you do it," she said.

"I keep telling you," I said.

"Oh right," she said. "You're a superhero."

"I'm superhero-ish," I said.

I heard Mr. Kensington honk outside. "I've got to go. Dad and Mr. Crow are waiting for me at the farm. We're launching the satellites tonight."

"Remember, you have school in the morning. Don't stay up too late."

I grabbed my bag and ran out to the car. Kensington opened the door, and I jumped in.

Mr. Crow was waiting with Dad when I arrived. We all walked into the hangar. Dad had already attached the satellite to the spaceship. It looked a lot like the ones we'd seen up in space but was much smaller.

"It's all ready to go," Dad said.

"Well, what are we waiting for?" I asked. "Let's launch a satellite."

I piloted the ship up to the level of LEO satellites, lower Earth orbits. They travel at a height of about 100 to 1,200 miles above the planet. We released the first satellite and then descended to get the second.

After that we traveled a bit higher to the middle-level satellites and released the second one. Finally, we lifted the third satellite to the high-level orbiting satellites. Mr. Crow explained that the companies he represented controlled about two hundred of the satellites in orbit.

My plan was that all the existing satellites that Mr. Crow's group controlled would receive information like always, but the information would also go through my new satellites. The new satellites would work like a filter. My program slowed everything down and made it easier to understand what was happening and where things were going.

Each satellite's data was tagged with a code so we could track it as it moved through the system. One of the reasons Mr. Crow's company couldn't track the thief before was because of the speed of their system. It was always churning out data and didn't have the ability to slow down and look at where the data was going or where it was being controlled.

I remotely turned on the satellites from my ship and they blinked to life.

"Can you really keep track of all this data and make sense of it?" Dad asked.

"I guess we'll find out. It's amazing how much

money is flowing invisibly right now through all these satellites. There are billions of dollars just floating in the air. I'm not surprised someone found a way to steal some of it. It looks like the data is flowing through the new satellite well. The question now is whether the thief will strike again."

We orbited all the satellites a little longer to make sure everything was operating correctly, and then headed back to Earth. I felt like a hunter setting a trap. Now I just needed to wait and see if I caught anything.

CHAPTER 20
The Hero Never Sticks Around

The next day the kids at school had finished programming all the satellites and entering the codes. We spent the day monitoring and looking for anything strange, but nothing happened. All the money made by the companies flowed as it was supposed to from the stores, to the satellites, to bank accounts.

I went home that day feeling discouraged. I had involved the school, I'd promised Mrs. Petty new computers for the whole district, and I'd promised Mr. Crow I'd catch the thief. The pressure was starting to really get to me by the middle of the next day. Kids were starting to look bored, and I could tell Mrs. Petty was nervous that the whole thing was a mistake. Then, on the third day, it happened.

All at once the money flowing from the stores to the satellites just vanished. It was like someone was doing an invisible magic trick—now you see it, now you don't.

"Benji, it's happening!" Mr. Crow said.

"I know," I said. "It's perfect."

"What do we do?"

"Nothing, for now just hold on and let the program do its magic. This is exactly what I wanted to have happen. My program is already slowing the data down and tracking the flow of the money. We'll know where it's going very soon."

The money kept disappearing. It would flow into the system of satellites and then disappear. As the data flowed in, the program slowed it down. Cindy broke it into chunks and sent it to the teams. The teams watched it in slow motion to see if the data flowed anywhere unexpected or if there was a gap in the flow.

At two forty-five, right before school was about to let out for the day, a girl in another sixth grade class shouted, "I've got it! I've got it!"

Cindy and I ran over. "What is it?" I asked.

"The satellite I'm tracking has a break in the code. A split second before the money goes into the bank a miniprogram appears for a fraction of a second and sends the money to another satellite."

"This is HUGE! All we have to do now is figure out who owns that satellite, and we've got our thief," I said.

I sat next to her and hopped on her computer. All the satellites orbiting the world are listed in a database. The database lists the registered owner of every satellite. I almost fell off the chair when my search returned the owner's name: Sir Robert!

"Do you see what I see?" Dad asked.

"I knew he had something to do with this," Mr. Crow said.

"I'm sure you did, Mr. Crow," I heard Sir Robert

say from behind us. We all turned in disbelief to see him standing in the doorway.

"Interesting timing," Mr. Crow said. "We were just about to call the police and have you arrested."

"By all means, call the police, but they won't be arresting me."

"Sir Robert," I said. "You own the satellite being used to steal money from Mr. Crow and his partners."

"You're right, Benji. I own the satellite, but I don't use it. I lease it to two associates of Mr. Crow. Isn't that right?" he said turning his attention to Mr. Crow's assistants. The looks on their faces said it all.

"Why didn't you say something sooner?" I asked.

"I almost did, but then I learned that you were on the case and knew it would be only a matter of time until you caught these two." He handed me a computer disk. "This contains all the information you'll need to have these two locked up."

Things were getting messy. I decided it was time to call the police. We had the data, and we knew where the money was going. The only thing left to do was sort all this out and arrest the thieves. Within minutes of making the call, the police and the FBI arrived at the school. There were sirens and flashing lights everywhere.

"Mr. Crow looked devastated. "This is going to be huge news and terrible publicity for my group."

"It'll be big news, but I don't think it has to be

all bad for your group," I said, noticing a long line of news vans streaming into the school parking lot. "When the reporters ask to talk with you, focus on the fact that you partnered with school kids to solve a complex computer problem. Talk about how the kids worked with satellites and programmed the computers to catch a theives. People will love the fact that you included kids."

"You'll have to join me to explain how you kids did it," he said.

"I'm not the one you want talking to the news people," I said, pointing to Cindy. "She is."

We explained to the police and gave them the data we'd collected. They arrested the two guys that had been stealing from Mr. Crow's companies.

Reporters gathered outside the school. Microphones stuck out in every direction. "I think we should go out and talk with them," I said.

We all went out, and they rushed over.

"Is it true your company was hacked and billions of dollars were stolen?" one reporter asked. Mr. Crow looked my way and winked. "Yes, that's true, but the thieves have been caught and the bigger story is our partnership with Principal Petty and the kids at her school," he said, waving Cindy and Mrs. Petty over.

It played out exactly how I'd expected. The reporters were more interested in the fact that a major computer company had partnered with a school to catch a hacker than the fact that the company had been robbed. Cindy explained to everyone how the school programmed and coded the satellites, and Mrs. Petty talked about how Mr. Crow's company agreed to donate computers to the entire school district.

I slipped around back and into the limo.

Sir Robert was already inside. "Benji, did you really think I was a thief?" he asked.

I felt pretty awful. Sir Robert was my mentor. I looked up to him in so many ways, but I had also doubted him. "I know it sounds crazy, but I did. I'm sorry. I should have known better."

"No need for an apology. If I were in your shoes I might have suspected me too."

"It looks like you've got quite the circus on your hands," Kensington said. "These reporters are going to want to talk with you too, you know."

"The hero never sticks around for a thank-you," I said. "Besides, I think I'm late for my cape fitting."

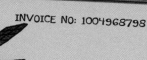

INVOICE NO: 1004968798

NOTICE OF PAYMENT

FROM: BENJI FRANKLIN
TO: MR. CROW

Fuel for spaceship	$175,000
Satellite delivery	$200,000
Total cost for project	$4,175,000
20% Consulting fee	$200,000
Total amount due	$4,375,000

PAID!

*2,000 computers No charge, supplied by Mr. Crow (Value $2,200,000)
*Satellite Supplied by Mr. Crow (Value $1,600,000)

PAYMENT DUE UPON RECEIPT

RAYMOND BEAN

Raymond Bean is the best-selling author of the Sweet Farts and School Is A Nightmare series. His books have ranked #1 in Children's Humor, Humorous Series, and Fantasy and Adventure categories. He writes for kids that claim they don't like reading.

Mr. Bean is a fourth grade teacher with fifteen years of classroom experience. He lives with his wife and two children in New York.